Other books by Mick Inkpen:

One Bear at Bedtime
The Blue Balloon
Threadbear
Billy's Beetle
Penguin Small
Lullabyhullaballoo!
Nothing
Bear
The Great Pet Sale
Baggy Brown
We are wearing out the naughty step

The Wibbly Pig books
The Blue Nose Island books

First published in 2006
by Hodder Children's Books

This edition published in 2010

Text and illustrations copyright © Mick Inkpen 2006

Hodder Children's Books, 338 Euston Road
London NW1 3BH

Hodder Children's Books Australia
Level 17/207 Kent Street
Sydney, NSW 2000

ISBN: 978 0 340 95658 8
10 9 8 7 6 5 4 3 2 1

Printed in China

Hodder Children's Books is a division of
Hachette Children's Books.
An Hachette UK Company.
www.hachette.co.uk

One year with Kipper

Mick Inkpen

Hodder
Children's
Books

A division of Hachette Children's Books

In **January**
Kipper took a picture with his new camera and made a New Year Resolution,

'This year I will not throw any snowballs at Tiger.'

And for a whole month he kept his promise. . .

Because the snow
did not fall until
February!

An icicle grew on
Kipper's house.
It lasted for three
weeks and grew
to 87 centimetres.
Kipper took a
photograph.

In March the wind flapped Kipper's ears.

It straightened his scarf and scruffled the daffodils on Big Hill.

Then it blew Tiger right off his feet!

Click!

This is the picture that Kipper took.

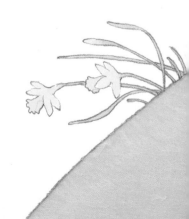

Soon the pond in the park was full of croaking and wriggling and glooping and jiggling. 'March is the froggiest month,' said Kipper.

'But April is best for catching tadpoles.'

By May there was blossom on the pavements thick enough to kick, and three ducklings in the park. One of them followed Tiger everywhere.

Quack!
Quack!
Click!

In June Kipper lay on his back and watched as little things with legs and wings climbed the spindly grasses and whizzed into the big, blue sky.

'There are a lot more little things with legs and wings than you would think,' thought Kipper.

The first week in
July was hot.
The second week
was hotter still.

And then Boom!

BOOOM!

BOOOM!

A thunderstorm!

August was
summer holiday time.

Kipper took a parachute
ride above the sea.

'Take my
picture!'
he called
to Tiger.

In September the bramble bushes were full of blackberries.

The thorns were prickly. 'Ouch! Ouch!' But the

blackberries were delicious.

'Mmmmmmmmm!'

In October

Kipper and Tiger made a collection of autumn things.

'October is an orangey-brown sort of month,' said Tiger.

They made a face from the pumpkin which glowed in the dark.

November

came around, and twiggy
branches made patterns
against the misty moon.

They huffed their breath
into the heavy garden air,
seeing who
could huff
the highest.

In December the days grew dark and cold.

Kipper stayed indoors making decorations and a special Christmas present for Tiger.

'I need one more photograph,' said Kipper.

So he called Tiger and got out his camera.

'Smile!'

said Kipper as he opened the front door.

But Tiger was already smiling – because it was snowing.

And because he had not forgotten about February.

Click! went Kipper's camera.

Booof!
went Tiger's snowball!

What we did this y...

...ary
February
March
May
June
July
September
October
November

April

August

December

Christmas

day came and Kipper
gave Tiger his present.
'Look at me in
August!' said Kipper.
But Tiger was
looking at December.
'This one is
the best!'
he said.